For my parents

Copyright © 1972 by David McKee
First published in Great Britain in 1972
First published in the U.S.A. in 1973
Library of Congress Catalogue Card Number: 76-6104
ISBN: 0 200 71893 2 Trade
0 200 71946 7 GB (USA only)
Published in Canada by Longman Canada Limited.

NEW YORK
Abelard-Schuman
Limited
257 Park Avenue So.
10010

LONDON
Abelard-Schuman
Limited
158 Buckingham Palace Road SW1
and
24 Market Square Aylesbury

Printed in Great Britain
by T. & A. Constable Ltd., Edinburgh

The Man Who Was Going to Mind the House

A Norwegian folk-tale retold and illustrated by

David McKee

Abelard-Schuman
New York   London

Ulrik, a very bad-tempered man, lived with his wife and baby in a small cottage close to a steep little hill. Although his wife cooked and cleaned and washed and scrubbed all day long, he was never satisfied. Whenever he was home he used to grumble and shout and stamp about the house.

One evening, after he had spent the day hay-making, Ulrik came home in an even worse temper than usual. As soon as he entered the house he shouted, "What a day I've had! My back's breaking! I've been working in the hot sun for hours while you've been here taking things easy. If you were a man you'd really know the meaning of work!"

His wife, tired of his grumbling, suddenly had an idea. "There's no need to lose your temper," she said. "We can change places. I can go and work in the fields while you stay at home and mind the baby."

"What a good idea!" Ulrik exclaimed. "I can do with a rest."

And so, early next morning, his wife strode off over the fields while Ulrik stayed at home. He finished his breakfast and sat back and watched the baby playing on the kitchen floor while he thought happily of the long, lazy day in front of him.

At last he got up and looked around to see what there was to do. He decided to churn the butter first but, as he worked, he became hotter and hotter. Churning, it seemed, was thirsty work. So down the cellar stairs he went and over to the beer barrel. As he turned on the tap, he heard the pig pattering about upstairs.

"The pig might upset the churn," he thought. He trotted quickly up the stairs and ran into the kitchen. He was too late! The churn was already overturned and the pig was licking up the cream.

Furious, Ulrik kicked the pig out of the house, but he kicked so hard that the pig fell down and lay there unconscious.

Suddenly he remembered the beer. He had left the tap running. He rushed down the stairs only to find that he was too late again. The floor was flooded with beer, and what was worse, the barrel was empty. Now he couldn't even have a drink.

He plodded slowly up to the kitchen and went to the larder for the rest of the cream to make the butter. Then he began to churn away as hard as he could for it was already nearly dinnertime and his wife would be expecting him.

Suddenly he clapped his hands to his head. He had forgotten the cow. Instead of taking her to the field he had left her in the cowshed, and he hadn't given her anything to eat or drink.

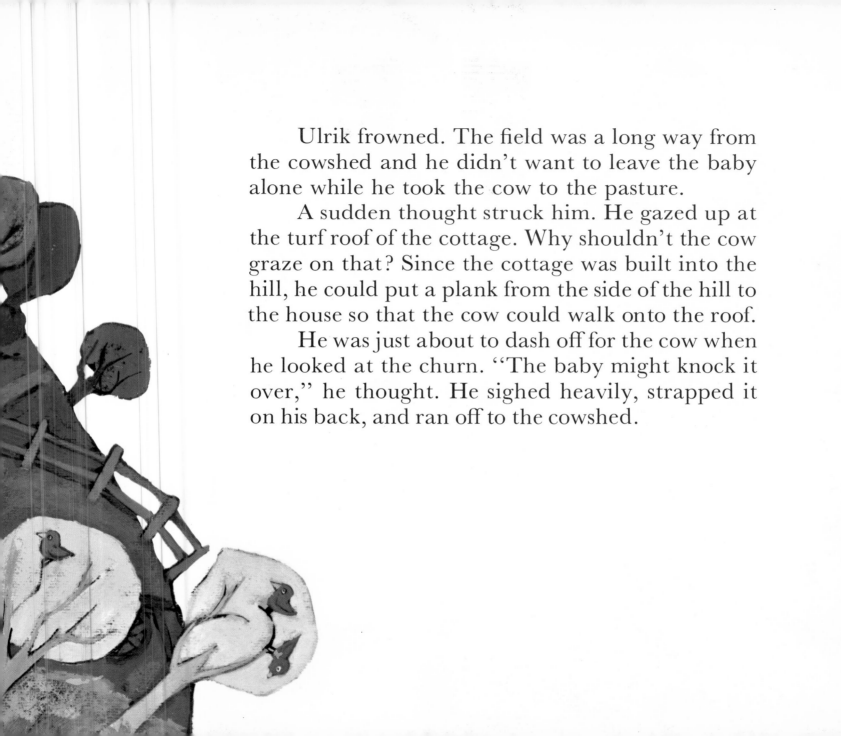

Ulrik frowned. The field was a long way from the cowshed and he didn't want to leave the baby alone while he took the cow to the pasture.

A sudden thought struck him. He gazed up at the turf roof of the cottage. Why shouldn't the cow graze on that? Since the cottage was built into the hill, he could put a plank from the side of the hill to the house so that the cow could walk onto the roof.

He was just about to dash off for the cow when he looked at the churn. "The baby might knock it over," he thought. He sighed heavily, strapped it on his back, and ran off to the cowshed.

The cow, tired of being shut up, followed him eagerly up the hill, across the plank, and onto the roof. As she began to chew the grass, Ulrik groaned aloud. She still had no water. He would have to go to the well and fetch some.

He left the roof, crossed the plank, went down the hill, and hurried into the yard. As he bent to pull up the bucket, the cream ran out of the churn, over his head, down his neck and splashed into the well. Ulrik groaned again. Now he wouldn't be able to make any butter at all since there was no more cream in the larder.

But they still had to eat, and so he scurried into the kitchen, hastily filled the cooking-pot with water, and hung it over the fire. They would have to have porridge for dinner.

Above his head he heard the cow moving around on the roof. "She might fall off and break her leg!" he thought anxiously. Picking up some rope, he rushed out of the house, up the hill, across the plank and onto the roof again.

Hastily he tied the rope round the cow's neck and flung the other end down the chimney. Back across the bridge he ran, hurtled down the hill, and galloped back into the house. As he rushed past the fire where the water was bubbling loudly, he threw in a handful of porridge and, panting breathlessly, picked up the rope which was dangling down the chimney and tied it tightly to his own leg.

As he stirred the porridge there was a strange noise overhead!

Then there was a thud. The cow had fallen from the roof!

Ulrik was dragged up the chimney by his leg—and there he stuck!

The cow was stuck too.
Neither of them could go
up or down!

Ulrik's wife, waiting in the fields for her husband to come and tell her their dinner was ready, became more and more impatient. At last she decided to go home on her own.

As she turned the corner, her eyes nearly popped out of her head. The poor cow was hanging over the edge of the roof and mooing pitifully. With one blow of her scythe she slashed through the rope. As the cow tumbled to the ground, Ulrik tumbled down the chimney.

Into the house she ran. "Ulrik! Ulrik!" she cried, but Ulrik didn't reply. He couldn't, for he was standing upside down in the chimney, his head stuck fast in the cooking-pot.